Dear Educators, Parents, and Caregivers,

Welcome to Penguin Core Concepts! The Core Concepts program exposes children to a diverse range of literary and informational texts, which will help them develop important literacy and cognitive skills necessary to meet many of the Common Core State Standards (CCSS).

The Penguin Core Concepts program includes twenty concepts (shown on the inside front cover of this book), which cover major themes that are taught in the early grades. Each book in the program is assigned one or two core concepts, which tie into the content of that particular book.

Pins & Needles Share a Dream covers the concepts Friendship and Problem Solving. This book can be used to expose students to the social-emotional concept Friendship, as recommended in the CCSS for Speaking and Listening. By learning appropriate behaviors for interacting with friends, students can develop important skills such as respect, caring, and cooperation. The concept Problem Solving can help students develop important cognitive skills necessary to meet many of the CCSS, such as how to apply problem-solving skills, engage creativity and imagination, and make predictions. After you've read the book, here are some questions/ideas to get your discussions started:

- In this story, Pins has a scary dream, and Needles has to comfort him. Discuss ways in which the children have been comforted by a friend, and times when they were the ones doing the comforting.

- One of the problems in this story is that Pins feels embarrassed because his quills have fallen out. Discuss the other problems in the story. How are the problems resolved?

- Ask the children to predict what will happen the next time Pins has a bad dream.

Above all, the books in the Penguin Core Concepts program have engaging stories with fantastic illustrations and/or photographs, and are a perfect way to instill the love of reading in a child!

Bonnie Bader, EdM
Editor in Chief, Penguin Core Concepts

Pins & Needles

SHARE A DREAM

For Joan, who shares
many dreams with me—SK

For Fay—KL

GROSSET & DUNLAP
Published by the Penguin Group
Penguin Group (USA) LLC, 375 Hudson Street, New York, New York 10014, USA

USA | Canada | UK | Ireland | Australia | New Zealand | India | South Africa | China

penguin.com
A Penguin Random House Company

Library of Congress Cataloging-in-Publication Data is available.

ISBN 978-0-448-46210-3 (pbk)   10 9 8 7 6 5 4 3 2 1
ISBN 978-0-448-48198-2 (hc)   10 9 8 7 6 5 4 3 2 1

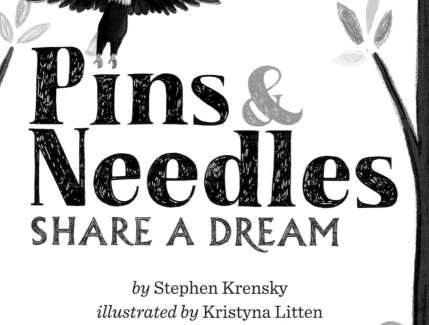

Pins & Needles
SHARE A DREAM

by Stephen Krensky
illustrated by Kristyna Litten

Grosset & Dunlap
An Imprint of Penguin Group (USA) LLC

Pins and Needles were best friends.
They liked to do things together.

But they didn't do anything
the same way.

When they played hide-and-seek, Pins always hid in the darkest place he could find.

Needles never found him there.
He was too scared to look in dark places.

One day Needles went to Pins's house for lunch.

"Hello!" said Needles, knocking on the door. But Pins did not answer.

Needles went to the window,
but he couldn't see inside.

Where could Pins be?

One time Pins was
stuck inside a log.
Maybe he was stuck again.
But the log was empty.

Next, Needles checked
the pond where Pins liked
to go swimming.

Needles saw two otters playing.
But he didn't see Pins.

Needles stopped to think.
Maybe Pins had gone out to gather
things for lunch.
Maybe he was home by now.

Needles pressed his ear against Pins's door.
He heard a noise from inside.
"Pins, I know you're in there," said Needles.
"Open up. It's time for lunch."
But the door remained shut.

"Go away," Pins called from inside.
"I have already done that," said Needles.
"Well, go away again," said Pins.

"Something is wrong," said Needles. "I can hear it in your voice."

"My voice says leave me alone," said Pins.

"At least tell me why,"
said Needles. "You can do
that through the door."

"All right," said Pins, "if you must know, I had a bad dream last night."

Needles shivered.
He hated bad dreams.
"What happened?"
he asked.

"I was climbing a tall tree," Pins explained.
"It was a long way to the top."
"Oh," said Needles, who only liked heights
when he was looking up at them.

"Suddenly," Pins went on,
"an eagle swooped down
and grabbed me."

Needles shuddered.

"The eagle dropped me into her nest," said Pins. "Then I saw a mountain lion nearby. He growled at me."

Needles shuddered some more. He had never met a mountain lion and wanted to keep it that way.

"The eagle SCREECHED."

The mountain lion ROARED!

Then they began fighting.
I wasn't sure who to root for
because I was worried the winner
was going to eat me."

"Oh, oh, oh, oh!" cried Needles,
who didn't like any of this at all.

"Then I woke up," said Pins.
"Thank goodness," said Needles.
"But I'm not brave like you, Pins.
Your story really scared me.
Can I *please* come in?"

Pins opened the door.

Needles looked at Pins.

And they tried not to laugh.

"That dream sure scared my quills off," Needles said.
"Mine too!" Pins said.

And the two friends stayed by each other's side
as their quills grew back in.